MONKEY WORLD

the Thunderbolt Express

MATTHEW PORTER

SASQUATCH BOOKS
SEATTLE

The Thunderbolt is about to depart from Bartlett station.

"All aboard!"
calls the Station Master.

There's Mayday the detective
and Oscar the magician.
Ms. Trixie and her pug dog Napoleon.

There's Fabulous Fred with his Flying Flea Circus. Billy Baxter the ventriloquist and Mono the inventor.

And there at the back
with the odd-looking luggage is
Jango Jenkins and his Dixieland Band.

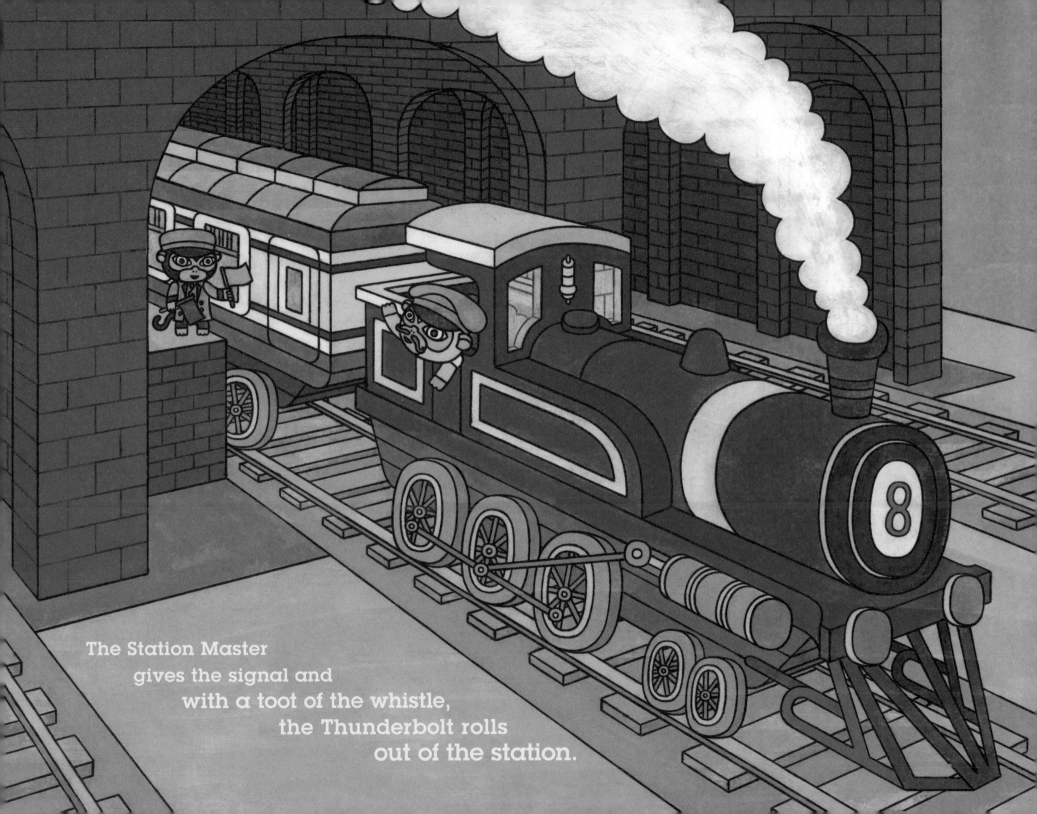

The Station Master
gives the signal and
with a toot of the whistle,
the Thunderbolt rolls
out of the station.

The train slips out of the city and into the country.
Past a farm with a windmill . . .

and a big red tractor.

Through hills covered with trees and fields full of flowers.

In the end carriage everyone
is having a marvelous time.

Jango Jenkins and his band are really swinging.
Only Mono the inventor refuses to jive.

Meanwhile, back in the compartment,
a mystery is unfurling.

"Napoleon is missing!" cries Ms. Trixie.
"Don't worry," says Mayday.
"I'll help you find him."

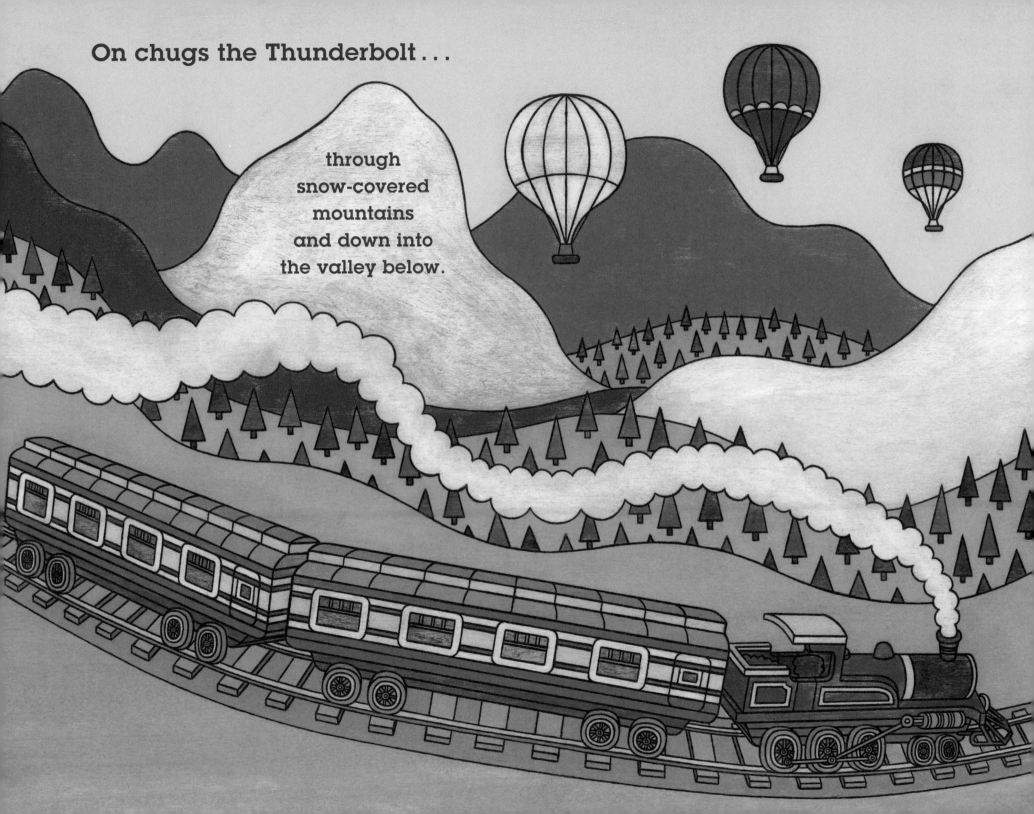

On chugs the Thunderbolt . . .

through
snow-covered
mountains
and down into
the valley below.

Then up front Herbert Smudge,
the engine driver, spots danger.

There is no bridge where
the bridge should be!

Herbert pulls the brake lever but it snaps off in his hand.
"Oh no!" he cries. Now there is no way to stop the train.

They'll fly off the track and plunge into the river.
And the river is full of crocodiles!

But all is not lost. Herbert has an idea.

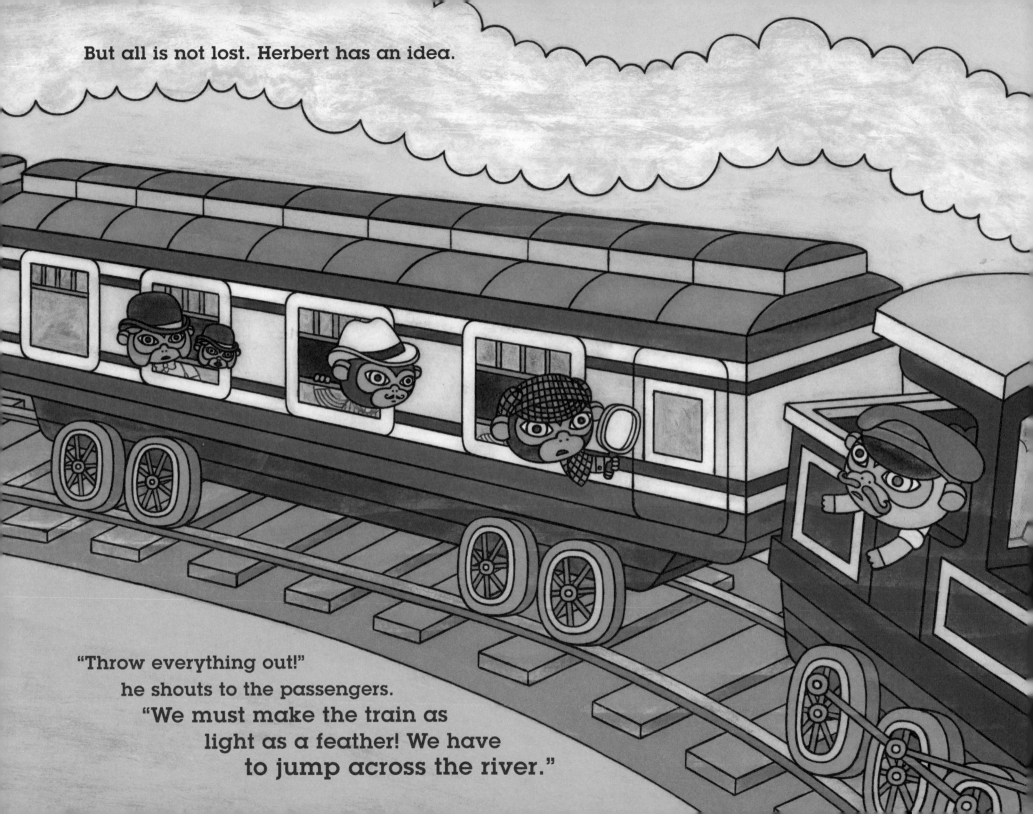

"Throw everything out!"
    he shouts to the passengers.
        "We must make the train as
            light as a feather! We have
                to jump across the river."

Oscar the magician flies into a panic.
He decides he would rather not be here at all.

He jumps into his vanishing cabinet
and Napoleon the pug appears.

Jango and his jazz band bid farewell to their instruments and Mono's robot flies away.

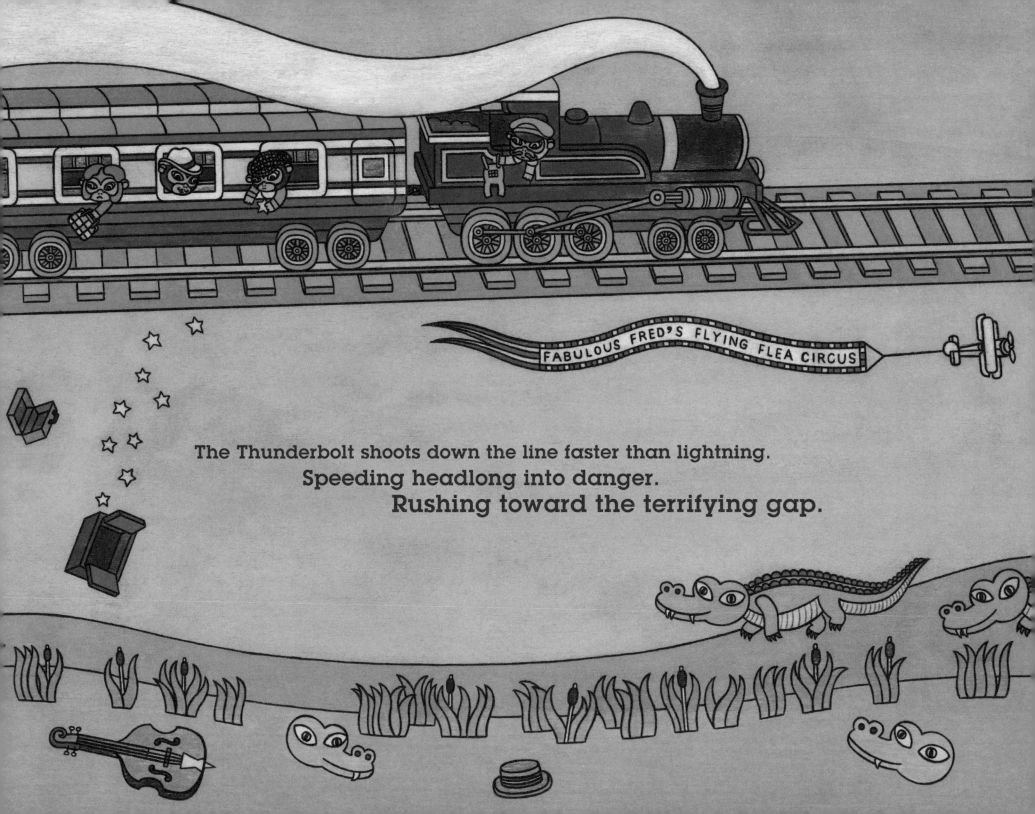

FABULOUS FRED'S FLYING FLEA CIRCUS

The Thunderbolt shoots down the line faster than lightning.
Speeding headlong into danger.
Rushing toward the terrifying gap.

"Hold on tight!" shouts Herbert
as the wheels leave the track.

FLYING FLEA CIRCUS

The Thunderbolt soars
through the air . . .

. . .and lands with a bump on the other side.
Everyone cheers. "We've made it!"

But not so fast! The brake is still broken. The Thunderbolt speeds on.

The train flips off the track going round a sharp bend...

and ploughs straight into a fairground.

Then it hops back on the track and into Miggleswick station where it glides to a halt alongside the platform.

"End of the line!" calls Herbert, as the passengers disembark.

Everyone cheers and all agree,
a few bits of luggage is nothing to pay for the
thrill of a ride on the Thunderbolt Express!

Meanwhile, back at the river, Oscar the magician finds himself in a tricky situation.

Perhaps it's time to disappear!

Manufactured in China by C&C Offset Printing
Co. Ltd. Shanghai, in June 2013

Published by Sasquatch Books
17 16 15 14 13   9 8 7 6 5 4 3 2 1

Editor: Gary Luke
Project editor: Nancy W. Cortelyou
Cover design: Anna Goldstein
Interior design: Sarah Plein
Illustrations: Matthew Porter

Library of Congress Cataloging-in-Publication
Data is available.

ISBN: 978-1-57061-877-2

www.matthewporterart.com

Sasquatch Books
1904 Third Avenue, Suite 710
Seattle, WA 98101
(206) 467-4300
www.sasquatchbooks.com
custserv@sasquatchbooks.com